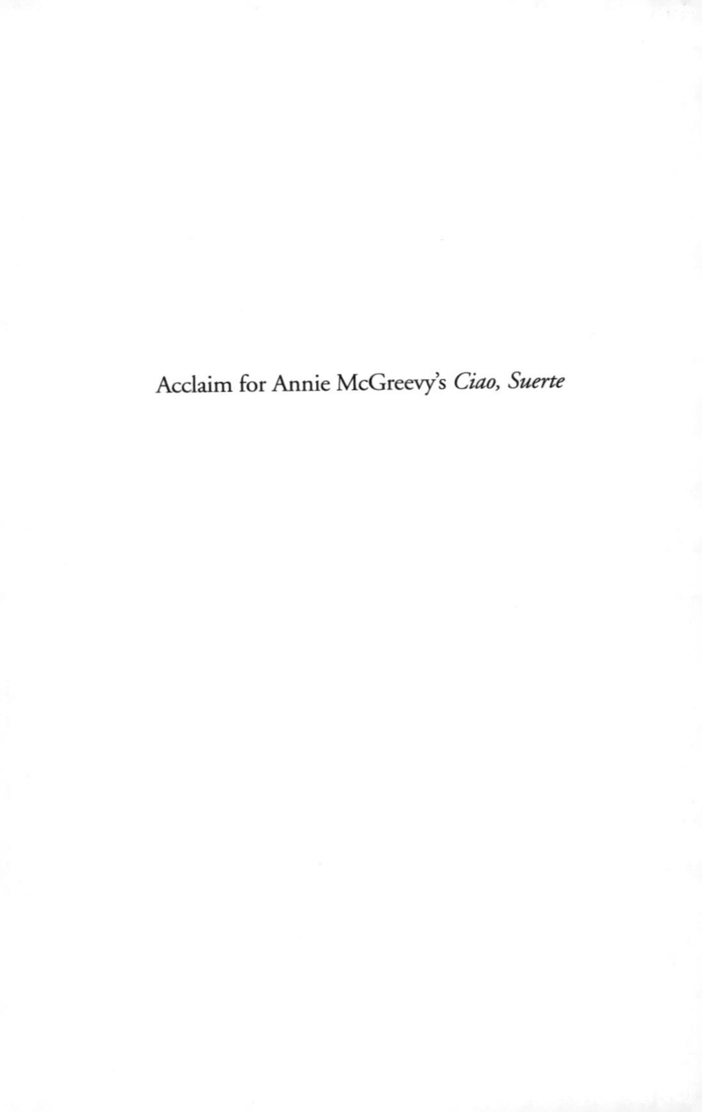

Acclaim for Annie McGreevy's *Ciao, Suerte*

"The first thing one notices—admires, envies, covets—about this novella is its audacious movement. Stretching back to Argentina's grim past, reaching forward to our own imperiled future, and pausing in the present for moments of stunning insight and precision, *Ciao, Suerte* assembles a mosaic of converging lives, each, in Annie McGreevy's perfect phrase, "full of losses, some mundane, some extraordinary." Heartbreaking and taciturn sentences spirit the reader from South America to Europe and back again, enumerating along the way the perils of family, country, terror, and love. This is the best book I've read in ages!"

Claire Vaye Watkins, author of *Gold Fame Citrus*

"*Ciao, Suerte* is so gracefully told, so nimble, so ambitious and yet so effortless, that it's hard to believe it's a debut. Annie McGreevy has written a fierce and beautiful book about identity, family, grief, politics, secrets, and love. It's profound and it sparkles. I loved it."

Edan Lepucki, author of *California*

"Annie McGreevy's novella beautifully collapses the presumed distinction between the personal and the political, the public and the private. The story unfolds with...immediacy. What emerges is a powerful, far-reaching story of tragic historical dimensions that touches on both the mutability of identity and the stubborn intransigency of blood ties. It is history given the flesh and bone of lived experience."

Kermit Moyer, author of *Tumbling*

NOUVELLA
2015

This is a work of fiction. Names, characters, places and incidents are either the product of the author's imagination or are used fictitiously, and any resemblance to actual persons, establishments, events or locales is entirely coincidental.

CIAO, SUERTE

A Nouvella book / published 2015

Design by Isabel Urbina Peña

For information go to:
nouvella.com

Printed in the United States of America.

First Edition.

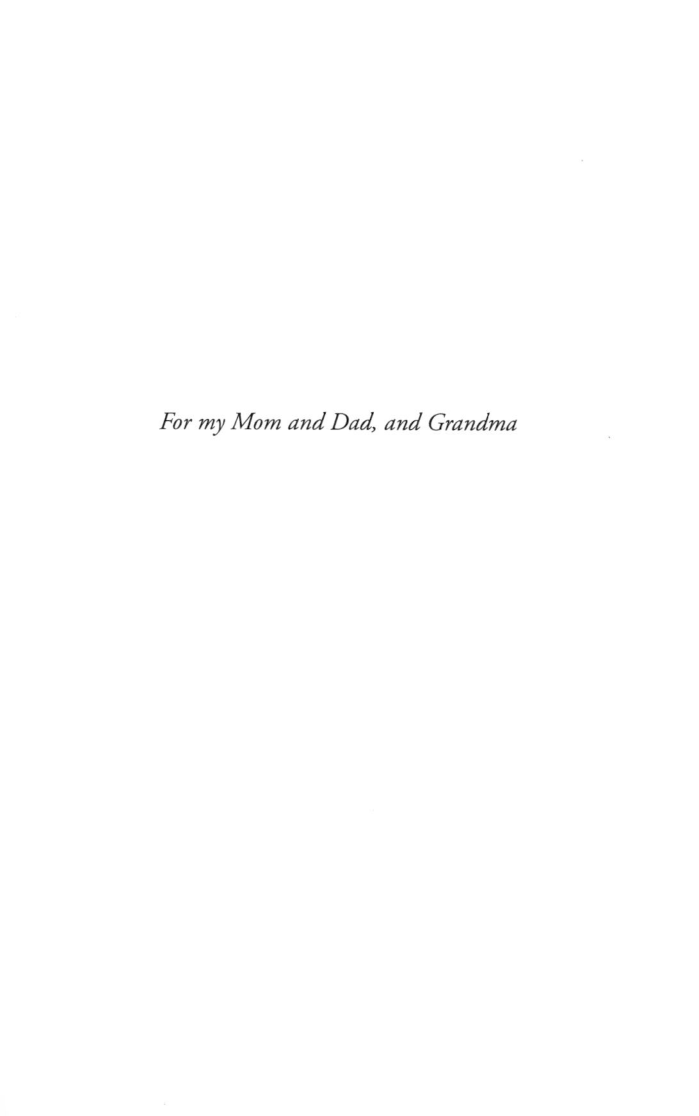

For my Mom and Dad, and Grandma

Ciao, Suerte

1

Children on the street in Rosario with Alejandro's white skin and floppy hair. A pre-adolescent volunteer at the hospital with Sabina's languid gait; a girl on television, competing in *Odol Pregunta*, with her posture. Sometimes Beatriz spends hours watching boys play soccer to see if any of them have her son's wooden legs or if their little faces redden with as much intensity as his did.

Children all over Argentina, it seems, who might be Beatriz's grandchild. There are hundreds, maybe thousands.

In 1990, she is at the Monumento de la Bandera when she sees a group of schoolchildren playing and a teacher trying to wrangle them into line to return to school. Out of habit, she scans them quickly with her eyes, but none of them remind her of her son or daughter-in-law. Then from behind her she hears

Alejandro's voice as it was when he was a child—throaty, high, full of urgency and mischief.

"*Espera*!" the voice calls. Wait up!

Beatriz spins around. A girl with dirty blonde hair is yanking her sagging knee socks and jogging to catch up to the group. She has an overconfident smile like the one Alejandro wore on his face until the day he was killed, probably, and the resemblance is so arresting that Beatriz actually reaches out and grabs the girl's arm.

"What is your name?" she demands. The name won't do her much good, Beatriz knows—she just wants to hear the girl's voice again. The girl looks startled, but otherwise unafraid. She eyes Beatriz with an air of conspiracy, as though she likes this old woman's boldness, and this—the fact that the girl seems begging for danger—is further reason to believe she could be Alejandro and Sabina's daughter.

She sticks her tongue out at Beatriz. A teacher appears.

"What do you think you're doing?" the teacher says as she pulls the girl free of Beatriz's grip.

Beatriz opens her mouth to respond, but the teacher interrupts.

"Go with your sister," she hisses to the girl. The girl slinks off and falls into line with another nearly identical to her; taller though, with the awkward hips and lumpy sweater of a body already playing a game of give and take with puberty. Impossible that she is Beatriz's granddaughter then, as Sabina's pregnancy when she was abducted was her first. And only. Beatriz mumbles an apology to the teacher and walks away.

* * *

There were other incidents before the girl at Monumento de la Bandera.

1984: Beatriz reads an article in *Clarín* in which General Ramón Camps tells the newspaper that he orchestrated thousands of murders and kidnappings. About the appropriation of newborns he says: *Subversive parents raise subversive children*. Beatriz's hands shake as she reads it, rage filling her. A system that she has never respected has killed her son for using his brain. For joining a group. For learning. All things Beatriz had encouraged him to do; things her own father had encouraged *her* to do. And now here was Camps talking—no, bragging about it on TV and in the newspaper. Alejandro and Sabina never killed anyone. They weren't criminals. All they'd done was join a group. After reading the article, Beatriz gets into bed and doesn't get out for over a week except to use the bathroom. The only other time she was still for so long was when she'd had her wisdom teeth removed as a teenager and her father said, *Think of it like four separate gunshot wounds inside your mouth.* That's what you're recovering from. Then he smiled. *Time to take a break from talking*, he'd teased. This is the same, Beatriz thinks now, thirty-five years later—it's like bleeding inside my own head. But this will never end.

1985: Beatriz submits a blood sample to the Grandparents' Index. The *Madres y Abuelas de la Plaza de Mayo* have support from abroad. They have powerful lawyers. Geneticists have taken an interest in their cause. They have found some adopted children of the disappeared and returned them to their biological grandparents. Beatriz is hopeful, and the hope pulses through her veins like a drug.

1986: Beatriz's husband Giancarlo increases his campaign to try to convince her that their grandchild was never born. The man who never gets angry loses his temper with Beatriz one night after dinner. "You were a nurse!" he booms. "Don't you know? They tortured her before they killed her. Pregnancy can't withstand that!"

Beatriz knows he's trying to spare her more pain. She knows he could certainly be right. But she can feel the slightest whisper of intuition telling her the opposite.

1988: Alejandro and Sabina are officially declared dead. Tell me something I don't know, Beatriz thinks.

* * *

One more low after the incident in the art museum:

1992: Giancarlo leaves Argentina for Italy, something he's been threatening to do for nearly thirty years. He tells her he's going one night as they lie in bed. "I can't stay here anymore," he says. "I'll die."

"We're dying anyway," Beatriz says, though they're not very old and have no real health problems. A cruel trick of nature, she thinks after their annual doctors' visits. Maybe we'll live forever. Maybe we'll outlive the grandchild and its grandchild and the next generation of holocausts.

"Don't you want to at least stay in our country?" Beatriz thinks that if their neighbors overheard them, they would think the two of them were discussing the weather, so drained of energy are their voices.

"It's not a country anymore. It's nothing."

Beatriz stares at the ceiling. She has been living in this house for almost forty years, since she married Giancarlo. On so many nights, she has watched him sleep soundly beside her while she stayed up fretting: when Alejandro was just a baby, colicky and scrawny and refusing her milk (he had to do things his way even then); when she miscarried their second and third and fourth babies; when Alejandro met Sabina and would disappear with her for weeks at a time, coming back skinnier and skinnier and spouting off Che Guevara and Marxist-Leninist ideology; when the two of them took up with the Montoneros. And tonight, too, her husband is warm beside her, with this decision he clearly made some time ago. He can see a life for himself across the ocean, Beatriz thinks. A life of safety and forgetting. A life in which Alejandro's picture is not on the mantle, in which he'll never hear his wife wake up in the night saying his dead son's name. The beginning of a new life for Giancarlo, and surely the end of something, but of what?

They'd first seen each other at the hospital when Giancarlo was finishing his residency. He'd been doing a round of night shifts in the pediatric ward, and there, too, was Beatriz, a nurse from a fine family. The rumor was that her father had raised his daughters like boys, had allowed them to go to university, taught them to shoot rifles in the country, and had even gotten Beatriz a job at this hospital. She was tall, handsome. Not exactly beautiful. A strange femininity that he couldn't put his finger on. He got into the habit of watching her study her charts, which she did with as much concentration and consideration as if she were the doctor. She was a conscientious assistant, her movements swift, exact. One day she assisted him when he performed an appendectomy on a teenage girl, and her presence had made him more nervous than the director's had. But it wasn't until they ran into each other at the tennis courts one morning that he formally introduced himself. The jacarandas were in bloom, everything smelling of lilac, and fallen purple petals had been swept to the sides of the courts. They'd make a good match, he knew, but as he began courting her, the intensity of his attraction surprised him. She seemed older than she was, like she had made her peace with the complexities of life, and he liked talking to her and listening to her. Best of all, in those first months, there would be times when he would forget what she looked like; he would search and search in his mind, but not be able to put together a face for her, not exactly, so every time she appeared it was like seeing her for the first time, each occasion a new pleasure.

Their engagement had been short and their wedding formal. Soon after, even before they found their rhythm as lovers, Giancarlo began to feel that Beatriz was an extension of his body, like there was something inside of her, just underneath her skin, that he needed every day. He could get it from standing next to her or looking her in the eye, hearing her voice. And her laugh—she laughed so loud when they were alone.

Giancarlo is thinking about that laugh now, how he hasn't heard it in decades, as they lay silently next to each other. He approaches it intellectually, because that's how he approaches everything. Sure, she still laughs. It just isn't like it used to be. When did he hear it last? Maybe when Alejandro was a teenager, comedic in his angst and over-seriousness? Maybe when Ale had met Sabina and joined the group and they would make jokes about it all to mitigate their worries? Giancarlo would like to put his finger on a date, an event, but he can't. He looks over at Beatriz, but she's closed her eyes.

They'd gotten pregnant right away, and her

pregnancy with Alejandro had gone smoothly. He'd been a cranky baby, but by the time he was two they were ready to try again. Getting pregnant didn't seem to be their problem. They'd always conceived within two or three months of trying. But when, six weeks into her second pregnancy, Beatriz bled so much she thought she was surely dying, she was devastated. They knew this happened all the time, that it was normal, even, but it still undid her. Giancarlo was there to soothe her. Half of being a good doctor, his mentor had told him, was having an organized mind. He'd arranged for his mother to take Ale (as they were calling him then) and he stayed home with Beatriz for three straight days, doing the cooking, holding her, all the while delivering kind, authoritative reminders that there was nothing wrong with her, that they would try again, that Ale would be a big brother soon enough.

The second time had been similar. Six weeks, the bleeding starting in the middle of the night, Giancarlo calm and Beatriz in pieces. She was twenty-nine and Ale was in school.

But the third one. It was something out of a horror movie. She was five months pregnant and it was at a doctor's appointment that they realized there was no heartbeat, and that even though her belly was continuing to swell, the child inside her had been dead for days, maybe even weeks. Giancarlo had been devastated, but the humiliation he felt at not noticing the absence of movement when he put his hand to Beatriz's belly three, four times day, was worse. They'd had to induce labor to extract the fetus, and while Beatriz was under anesthesia, Giancarlo had stayed in the room. He saw the fetus, half the size of a newborn baby, but fully formed, with purple bloated skin. A girl. She wore an expression that was half anguish, half disgust, as though she had fought whatever force that had tried to end her short life and died disappointed he had not done his part, that he had not understood how to save her.

The gynecologist who performed the procedure asked him if he wanted to hold the dead child, and he'd accepted only because he was speechless. The moment he spent with her in his arms was the most alarming of his life. It drove his own mortality into him worse than the death of his father would a decade later, and for months afterwards he directed his life with the intuition of an animal in winter.

It took Beatriz much longer to recover. By then, Ale was a chatterbox, a know-it-all with weak hand-eye coordination, exercise-induced asthma, and a penchant for memorizing things. For Beatriz he would perform the list of all the dinosaurs he knew, for Giancarlo every major city in Italy, all the bones of the body, the periodic table of elements, the names and statistics of every football player from Rosario, from Milan, from Saõ Paolo, and on and on and on. Giancarlo poured his energy into the boy, helping him with his homework, teaching him tennis, developing exercises for him to improve his athleticism and to alleviate his asthma. A year after the miscarriage he knew they would not have another child, and his love for Ale grew wilder. He became overprotective, proud of things that were not achievements. His only heir. The tragedy stripped him of his reason. He was more in love with his son than he had ever been with his wife.

Soon Beatriz was ready to try again, but by then Giancarlo had a plan. He learned her menstruation and tracked it on a calendar he kept in his locker at the hospital. It was simple. He didn't initiate lovemaking, and gently rejected her advances when it was possible for her to get pregnant.

Soon, Giancarlo was attending conferences in Europe two, three times a year, and Ale had grown into a surly teenager who talked relentlessly about national politics, a topic Giancarlo found distasteful and fit only for dilettantes and armchair intellectuals.

The boy kept changing, growing angrier and less and less like himself. Giancarlo wanted to be mad at him, to be disappointed even, to threaten him. But he never could. He turned into one of those men he used to pity, hopelessly in unrequited love with a careless person. But Giancarlo never gave up hope that all of it—Sabina, dropping out of school, joining the group—was just a phase, and that soon enough he'd grow out of it and into the man Giancarlo wanted him to be.

The problem, Giancarlo thinks now, as he turns off the lamp on his nightstand and turns his back to Beatriz, is this country. With its dictators worse than those his parents had left Italy to escape. It made scrambling fools of even the best men. It turned women like Beatriz into—what did she think she was? A private investigator?

Once you knew the problem, the solution was never far behind, and the exactness of the solution to the problem of Argentina and Beatriz finally relaxes him: Valentina, Italy. A distant cousin of his he'd first made love to at fifteen. A trail of embarrassing divorces and dysfunctional children had unraveled behind her in the fifty years since. He'd gone back to her every now and then out of curiosity or stress or pity. He used to regard her as desperate, even pathetic. But sometime after her final divorce, the same time he retired and found himself staring across the table into Beatriz's intensity far more often than he cared for, he began to see her as a way out. There was something comforting about her vulnerability, her self-deprecation. A peace to the low stakes of her life. She had been making room for him in her place in Bergamo for the past year, since they began making serious plans for him to leave.

He closes his eyes. *Valentina*, he says in his head, like a prayer. It will be good; it will be fine. He has come to the end of the line with Beatriz, with Argentina. But now everything must rearrange itself inside his imagination. Now it will be Valentina he lives with, sleeps with, touches every day, sees with her hair wet. And it will be Beatriz who exists only in his mind. It was a painful adjustment to relegate Alejandro to that space. The most difficult thing he ever had to do. But there is no room in his imagination for this mythical grandchild. Now, at the very least, Beatriz's obsession with finding it will cease to infect the last years of his life. Giancarlo doesn't want there to be a child—he hasn't wanted there to be one for years. He just wants to start over.

"I want you to come with me," Giancarlo says. But he doesn't turn to face her. The invitation is a gesture. He knows that she'll never leave Argentina until she finds the child.

* * *

And then—unexpectedly, miraculously—she does. It's 2003. Beatriz is seventy-two years old. She is aging slowly, to her disappointment. She is sitting in her apartment when the phone call comes. It's Mariela, the head of the *Madres y Abuelas*. A boy in Patagonia has been tested, and he is a match for Beatriz. They've found her grandson.

"*Un niño*," Beatriz says. All this time, she'd never been able to guess the child's sex with any certainty. Imagining a girl, imagining a boy, always felt wrong.

"*Un niño*?" Mariela's voice sounds harsh over the phone. "He's twenty-three years old."

"I know how old he is," Beatriz says hastily. "Where is he? When can I see him?"

"*Tranquila*," Mariela says. "We have his information, and we're going to give it to you. But you have to be patient."

"I've been patient for the last two decades. I want to see him."

"It's complicated. He didn't consent to being tested—he didn't even know he was being tested for anything besides steroids—and his parents have no idea. He's an amateur athlete." Mariela sighs from her desk in Buenos Aires and Beatriz presses her.

"What? How did you find out then? How can you be sure?"

"An *Abuela* working here at headquarters was sure a boy on the National Polo team was hers. She was wrong. But the entire team's samples were tested and run against the Grandparents' Index. That's how."

Beatriz can't catch her breath. She stops pacing around her apartment and sits down at the dining room table. "What does this mean? Can I meet him?"

"I can't tell you any more over the phone. Can you come to Buenos Aires?"

A few hours later, Beatriz is in Mariela's office, a bag packed. She plans to leave Buenos Aires for wherever the boy—man, she corrects herself—is.

What they did was illegal, Mariela begins. They had to pay their way out of it. Luckily, the assistant coach, whom the Abuela had bribed in the first place, was able to be bribed again, this time for Beatriz's sake. The organization was, of course, committed to the justice of reuniting grandparents with their biological grandchildren. But if Beatriz wanted to show her gratitude, a donation would certainly be appreciated.

2

Eduardo has been in an old folks' home for a long time, though he's only in his sixties. He began losing his mind bit by bit in the years after he was demoted from Lieutenant in 1973, after humiliating himself and his team in a street fight with terrorists. Those were the words used on the official document stripping him of his title, salary, and decorations: *humiliated, street fight, terrorists.*

Eduardo still has the document, folded into a small square and buried at the bottom of his underwear drawer, here in his little room in the home for the elderly, subsidized by the Argentine government. They give with one hand and take away with the other, but he's all right with the contradictions. He's been around; he's no naïf.

He takes out the document and looks at it from time to time, staring at the words on the paper. The language is all wrong. *Street fight.* Please. They weren't some kids with broken bottles. The terrorists had machine guns. That made *him* incompetent? Looking at the document used to infuriate him, but now he likes looking at it because it reminds him of the bottom. How he came up out of it. He'd started to feel cloudy in the head directly after they took his uniform away, but after a few months shuffling around the ministries in various capacities (the government, in the end, was generous with him, he knew this), he saw that he could still make himself useful to his country. He found himself working in recruitment, fund-raising, Veterans' Affairs. When the Malvinas war began, he was put on fundraising duty full time. He wrote letters to potential investors: philanthropists in Israel; conservatives in Colombia; business-men in Buenos Aires. He'd had the good luck to know Videla at the military academy when he'd been a young man, had supported the coup and removal of the silly woman president who had not even been able to follow the simple instructions left to her by Perón, and now that Videla was president, Eduardo had landed a job working on adoptions by military personnel and friends of the government.

There had been so many children born to unfit parents, young people with no jobs, no money, some of them downright degenerates, poor souls who were lost and practically children themselves. Those Marxist groups were no place to raise a child. He remembers the first baby he placed with a clarity that almost startles him: Mauricio. In Rosario, June 1977. He was born of a young, young girl—she looked almost too young to have a baby—and afterwards little Mauricio had to stay with her in her cell so he could be fed. The baby cried at night sometimes, Eduardo remembers, but it was a nice cry. Soon the girl was sick, and was to be transferred. They didn't want the baby to catch her illness, so they had rushed to find him a home. The girl had done something awful against the state, though now Eduardo can't remember what it was. And she was sick, terribly sick, but still had to be subdued by two officers when they took Mauricio away from her. What had landed her there in the first place? Had she killed someone? Thrown a grenade at an officer? He can't remember. And of course he doesn't tell all of this to his buddies when they're playing truco at the table after dinner. He tells them how he got to hand Mauricio to his adoptive parents—a lieutenant in the Navy and his wife, who was infertile—and how that felt. How the lieutenant's wife had cried. How they'd smoked a cigar after signing the papers. How for the first time in years Eduardo felt like himself again. How he got his mind back just a little bit with Mauricio and couldn't wait to do it again.

And the wives. They were so grateful they sometimes wrote him the most beautiful letters of gratitude, updating him on the child who had begun to walk or who had called them *Mamá*. At a certain point he was advised to burn the letters, and he did, but sometimes as he's sitting through a boring movie in the common room or an uncomfortable visit with the nurse, he extends the letters, imagines what those children are up to now.

Today, as the nurse takes his blood, as she runs her fingertip along his forearm looking for a fat vein, Eduardo thinks of Luisa and Elena, twins born in the same detention center in Rosario as little Mauricio, just a few months after: Luisa, the elder, teased Elena mercilessly as children, and it wasn't until they went through puberty that they became best friends. Now they're inseparable and live next door to each other.

Horacio, a surprisingly chubby, healthy one born

via Cesarian section out of a half-dead woman terrorist in Buenos Aires on January first, 1978: he grew up to be a professional soccer player. His healthy birth was a genuine miracle. And what a life he led! He traveled to Europe and played for Manchester United. He learned English tolerably well, but never lost his accent, which made him sound charming to the Brits. Eduardo chuckles to himself, thinking about Horacio. He got injured, and moved into coaching. He married and returned to Argentina. He lives in a big house in Banfield and takes care of his aging parents with his wife and children.

Antonella (Buenos Aires, 1980, the child of a detainee and a guard she'd been with) was the first girl in the family that adopted her to go to college. She became a scientist.

Gustavo (Cordoba, 1978, blonde) had always been a little bit of a faggot and loved to cut hair. He became a premier hairstylist for Argentine cinema. He was offered jobs in Hollywood and Bollywood, but refused them because he loved his country so much.

He shakes his head. What a time to live in. What an adventure it is to be alive. People were so amazing, and there were a million different ways to love them, even the ones you didn't know. People you'd never met—you could still change the course of their lives forever. Like those kids. Those kids! He shook his head again.

The nurse leaves and Eduardo has the rest of the morning to himself. His wife doesn't visit him in the home. Of course not. She took up with some asshole who never got his hands dirty. She gave up on Eduardo when the military did. It still hurt. Eduardo would call and she wouldn't talk to him. For a while, after he'd been demoted, with his wife not talking to him and not letting the girls talk to him either, he thought his body would stop. But things got better, as they always do.

Eduardo knows he doesn't have too much time left. He stands up out of his chair and goes into the bathroom, where his only mirror hangs. Wrinkled cheeks, bald head, soft belly. It's undeniable. But he has nothing to be ashamed of.

3

While Beatriz goes through customs at Ezeiza and Eduardo dozes his way through a medication-enhanced nap in the retirement home, across the Atlantic and above the equator, Miguel is falling in love.

He is staying with his brother Lautaro, living it up in Madrid. In the months before, almost done with university in Argentina, he had decided to switch tracks and study law, and so he would have to start from zero. But not yet; first, he would take a year off. His plan was to stay only a month, and then backpack around Europe. But the fun in Madrid is endless and if he stays through the spring, he and Laucha can backpack together.

The boys slept into the early afternoon and ate huge lunches at the Italian-Argentinean restaurant around the corner from Lautaro's place; they went to the Filmoteca four rainy autumn nights in a row and watched German movies with subtitles. They botellóned in the Plaza de San Ildefonso, smashing the bottles on the cobblestones after they finished them.

They met girls, lots and lots of girls. A chubby girl with a face so pretty she was hot anyway. Loud girls who guffawed with delight at the boys' accents. One of these fun-loving girls, a gorgeous redhead, went down on Miguel one night between two Peugeots on the Calle Pez. Another unintentionally imitated his Argentine pronunciation—turned her *ya*'s into *zsa*'s—which Lautaro had warned him would be annoying, but instead it cracked Miguel up.

They traveled, too. They went surfing in Cantabria, snowboarding in Navarra. They went to Granada and smoked a joint before taking a guided tour of La Alhambra, which they giggled through so disruptively that the guide asked them to leave. They busted out into the October heat and collapsed onto the grass, imitating the pedantic guide and laughing until their stomachs were sore.

By All Saints Day at the beginning of November, Miguel and Lautaro were tired and had spent more money in the previous three months than they had budgeted to get them to December. Miguel was deciding whether or not to hang out in Madrid all year or travel, as he initially planned to, when he met Inés on the hip-hop floor of Pacha.

She bumped into him and said, "*Perdona.*" She looked up at him and smiled, didn't move past him. She had long shiny brown hair and a freckled face smiling above a big chest and slim legs extending out of a pair of wool winter shorts.

"No problem," he said.

"What's your name?"

"Miguel," he said. "*Y vos?*"

She perked up at the word "*vos.*" "Are you Argentine?"

"I'm from Patagonia."

"*Alá!*"

She told him her name. They kissed each other on both cheeks. He bought her a drink. She told him about herself: Madrileña, student, business marketing, twenty-one.

He asked her if he could kiss her. She said yes. They kissed. He asked her to come home with him. She said yes. They kissed for a while on Lautaro's couch. He didn't feel the urge to try to move things along, which surprised him. They were both fully clothed when the sun came up.

"*Madre mía,*" Inés said. "I have to go home."

He asked her if he could take her home. She said yes. She leaned into him on the metro and when they reached her neighborhood, Canillejas, they climbed the stairs up to the sidewalk and she pointed across the highway to where she lived.

He said, "Let's stand on the bridge and watch the sun rise."

"We say goodbye here," she said.

Miguel cocked his head to one side.

"My father will be coming across that bridge soon, or getting onto the highway from there." She pointed to the on-ramp.

"Can I call you?" Miguel asked.

"Yes," she said. They exchanged numbers. Before two weeks had passed Miguel and Inés were inseparable and his decision was made. Madrid for the year it was.

4

Miguel is lying on Lautaro's couch with his head on Inés' lap, tracing a Polo field into her palm. He's been going on and on about the sport, how smart the horse is, how it knows to follow the ball without you telling it. How much he misses playing.

Inés is falling into something with Miguel. She's not sure it's love, but it's definitely something.

"Tell me something else about your life," she says to him. "I want to know the whole story. Day by day."

"That may be difficult." He laughs and looks up into her eyes. "Even I don't know everything. I'm adopted."

Inés' eyes widen. "*Adoptado*!" she cries softly. Inés' father is a *gato*, which means he was born in Madrid, unlike the millions of people who have come from villages in the last decades. Inés rarely has a day when she doesn't run into some member of her extended family on the street or the metro. They are atwitter with gossip about her new boyfriend, rumored to be tall and handsome and wealthy, and they won't leave her alone about him.

What must this boy's life have been like? she wonders. With parents so old, out in the wilderness, not a biological tie in the world? "And your brother?" she asks. "Is he adopted, too? Are you…blood related?"

Miguel shakes his head. "He's adopted from another mother. After me." He has soft gray bags under his eyes, which are heavy with sleepiness. "That's why we look so different," he says. "I look like my parents. They're both light like me. And tall. But it's a coincidence."

He trails off there, yawning—he doesn't seem interested in going into the details of his adoption. Inés is disappointed. She has a sister and a brother, and though there are two years between each of them, they look like triplets. They all still live at home, and they all look exactly like their mother. Baby pictures and voices on the archaic answering machine are indiscernible. Even their mother can't remember which one of them was the good sleeper, which one was a little pig at her breast, which one skipped crawling and went right to walking.

But it is the petty manifestations of their sameness that annoy Inés the most. For example: their farts all smell the same. And: Inés and her sister Julia share a room and they both talk in their sleep. Sometimes they wake up at the same time telling the other one to shut up. "*Calla*!" they say at the same time, and then Julia, who is a clown, giggles and Inés has to tell her to shut up again. Once, when Julia went to the village without her, Inés woke up in the middle of the night to the sound of herself talking and sat up and said, "Julia, do you *mind*?" only to find Julia's bed empty. The revelation that she was as much of a nuisance as her little sister made her fall back onto her pillow with a thud.

And so Inés is fascinated with these Argentine brothers, this thick one and this skinny one, and how they seem inseparable. She can't imagine what it would be like to look across the dinner table at her brother and not see her own face.

Miguel has picked up again—he's going on about elk hunting in Sweden with his father and Lautaro when he was a teenager.

"Elk!" Inés shrieks.

There were Welsh nannies, an entire room for video games. There was a brief bout of psychotherapy when he entered adolescence and had a problem with authority. He puts the word "*problema*" in scare-quotes and Inés reaches for his finger and pulls it to her lips. She kisses it softly, lingers there. Miguel pauses.

"Go on," she whispers. There was a big house in the country with six bedrooms. Miguel was a good Polo player, a decent snowboarder and a bad hunter. His parents were older, he said.

"How old?" Inés wants to know.

"My dad just turned seventy-four." Inés gasps. "And my mom's…sixty-five? Sixty-six? Yes. Sixty-six."

"That's not so old," she says, though her own parents' hair is not yet gray.

Miguel takes a deep breath and props himself up on his elbow. Inés doesn't want to push, but she can't help herself. "Do you know anything about your birth parents?" she asks.

"Not really," Miguel says. "Lots of people are adopted, you know." He looks up at Inés. "Even in Europe," he says, in a sing-song way that betrays his annoyance at her questions. He lies back down, returns his head to her lap.

It's more or less the truth. Miguel's known he was adopted for as long as he can remember. His father didn't like to talk about it, but his mother had read him and Laucha children's books about it, told them how they were just tiny little lentil beans, less than a week old each, when they chose them. She'd always emphasized that word, *chose*, as though she'd gone shopping for them and selected the best.

Of course, there had been things about it they could not ignore. Lautaro hitting puberty and turning into The Hulk, while Miguel continued resembling their parents in build and coloring, like the three of them belonged to the same TV family but Lautaro couldn't pass. That had jarred Miguel a little, and he knew kids at school sometimes teased Laucha about it.

The two of them had talked about it exactly once, a few months before Miguel was to leave for university. Lautaro had broken his leg at a rugby tournament and was out of after-school sports. One night he limped to Miguel's room after their parents had gone to bed. He stood in the doorway, his frame blocking most of the light from the hallway.

Miguel was lying on his stomach on his bed. He looked up from his magazine and saw something in his brother's face. He asked what was up.

"I was wondering," Lautaro started. He scratched at his nose with his knuckles. "Do you think it's possible that our biological mothers..." He let the question trail off. Miguel looked at him only for a moment before returning to his magazine. He flipped a page.

"During the stuff that was happening around the time we were born—" Lautaro tried again.

"What are you talking about?" Miguel asked, though it came out of his mouth not as a question seeking an answer, but as a demand intended to silence, a tactic of his father's. The man was an expert at shutting down conversations he didn't want to have.

Lautaro stared back at him, his face oddly neutral.

"You have too much time on your hands, man," Miguel said, kinder now.

Laucha swallowed and Miguel could see it and hear it. He cocked his head to one side as if contemplating a follow-up question, but Miguel got there first: "When did the doctor say you could go back to practice?"

"Another month."

"That sucks," Miguel went on. "To miss the whole end of the season. You're going to have to spend all summer getting back in shape."

"I'll be in physical therapy," Lautaro said.

"Physical therapy," Miguel concurred. He flipped through a few more pages without looking at them, and then closed the magazine and looked at Laucha as if to say *All done*.

But Laucha stayed where he was. "So you've never asked Mom or Dad about it?" His face curious and innocent.

Miguel balked. "Of course not. Are you crazy?" He stood up, stretched his arms over his head. He was taller than Laucha, but his brother had an easy fifteen kilos on him, most of it muscle. Even with his leg in a cast Laucha could take any of their friends or classmates. Of course they'd rough-housed as kids, they were competitive athletes, but fighting in real life wasn't in either of their natures. And yet in that moment Miguel wanted his brother to leave the room and to stop this line of questioning so badly that he would force him if he had to. He imagined himself pushing his brother down, subduing him. Something he hadn't done in so long he couldn't even remember.

But he didn't do this. He took two slow steps toward Lautaro, looking him in the eye. His brother took a step back, the hierarchy of their birth order intervening on their behalves.

"Mom would lose it," Miguel said, simply. "And Dad would be pissed, too."

Lautaro nodded. He left the doorway, and it took

Miguel a minute to slow his breathing. He felt a mixture of pride and shame.

This was the problem with Lautaro, he told himself as he readied for bed. He didn't understand that over time, boys grow into men and that it is their parents who needed to be protected from certain things. That there were things to say out loud, and things not to. Sure, they could be curious, they could wonder, but Miguel had no intention of making trouble.

He had underestimated Lautaro's persistence, though. The next evening, Miguel was sitting on the couch when he heard Laucha ask their mother about it as she was preparing dinner in the next room. The sound of her chopping ceased and she called for Miguel; he felt unable to move. He loathed his brother for doing this just as Miguel was leaving for university. She called him again. He came and stood in the doorway of the kitchen.

"We never met either of them," she said. She'd turned away then, as if to do something to the pot on the stove, but there was nothing more to be done. She had tried to prepare herself for this moment; she had rehearsed these words in her head. "Some young women, especially those who grow up in the country, have very, very difficult lives, and—"

"We're from the country?" Lautaro asked.

"The adoptions went through the archdiocese in Buenos Aires," she explained. Miguel knew that already. So did Lautaro. They knew as much of the story as they ever would. "We don't know exactly where you were born." She said this sadly, as if it pained her that she could not picture the room. Which it did. She had been waiting for this day in a kind of low-grade panic since she had become a mother.

Linda focused her eyes on Lautaro. She could see he had more questions. Miguel's eyes rolled toward the ceiling, like the entire conversation bored him. This refusal to disrupt his idea of their family overwhelmed her with affection for her stubborn son. But she was moved by Lautaro's curiosity, too, and she wanted to satisfy it, to do everything she could for him. She readied herself for what he would say next. If either one wanted to look for his biological parents, she had planned to support that, though she knew it would be nearly impossible. There had been no information about Miguel's mother—only that she had fair coloring similar to hers and her husband's, and had come from "good stock," as the archdiocese had put it. About Lautaro's adoption a few years later they'd only been told that his mother was practically a child, and that she was leaving the country immediately. Linda didn't like to think about it, but privately she felt that they were both dead.

* * *

When Miguel thinks of this conversation now, he doesn't find it particularly interesting. He doesn't even remember the details very well. Inés is looking at him expectantly, and he reflects on her very pretty face for a moment. He likes walking down the street with her, seeing her naked, likes how she's more comfortable and experienced in bed than he is, but never makes him feel inferior. He likes the sound of her voice and the way she speaks, although she sometimes sounds less than intelligent. But he's not wild about her questions.

He sums up that conversation in his parents' kitchen in Patagonia so long ago in a soundbite: "It all goes through the Church there. It was closed."

Inés doesn't know anything about any of this. When she thinks of Argentina, she thinks of the tango, yerba mate, their charming way of speaking, her favorite song by Andrés Calamaro. Now that she knows Miguel, she thinks of him in his big house in the cold south. She doesn't know about Argentina's history and doesn't know or care anything for politics.

What does she know? That she's terrified for the day seven months from now when Miguel will return to Buenos Aires. She hopes something big will happen before then—that he'll ask her to go back there with him, which she would be willing to do. It sounds corny inside her head, but her heart will follow him to Argentina anyway, so her body might as well go too. She looks down at him face up in her lap.

"Your stomach is growling," he says. "Do you want to go get some food?" He lets out another huge yawn and Inés worries that she's boring him.

She shrugs. She hadn't realized she was hungry. "Do you?"

He nods exaggeratedly. "I'm dying of hunger," he says. He stands up and stretches his skinny limbs.

"You look like it," Inés teases.

"*Calla*," he says. Shut up. He pulls her close and hugs her. "We can get something for Lautaro, too. He'll be back from his exam in a few hours."

Inés nods. "It's cold out," she says. "You'll need more than your sweatshirt."

Miguel shifts his weight from one foot to the

other, rocking Inés back and forth with him. "Thanks for the advice," he says, smiling. "But I'm from Patagonia."

* * *

Miguel and Inés are winding up the Calle Libertad when they see, coming out of a bar wearing a white coat and looking gorgeous, the redhead Miguel hooked up with between the two Peugeots when he first arrived.

"Ey, Miguel," she calls to him, "*Que tal*?" So casually. These European girls had no shame. That was part of what made them so attractive.

He can't remember her name. "*Hola*," he says. He can feel his face making itself into a smile and doesn't try to stop it. She is alone.

Inés looks at him. She looks at the girl. The girl looks at both of them. They are all breathing the same air. No secrets. The girl raises her eyebrows and bursts out laughing. She holds up a hand, waving at Miguel and Inés. "*Hasta luego*," she calls, turning away.

He stands looking at her as she walks down the street.

Miguel and Inés are still for a moment, neither

one speaking, and then they start walking again.

"Who was that?" Inés finally asks.

"Nobody," Miguel says. "Some girl I met through my brother. I don't even know her name."

"Then why did you look at her like that?" Inés asks. "You've been yawning all afternoon. I saw the way you perked up when she came out of there."

Miguel exhales. "We had a good time a while back. What's the big deal?"

"*Had a good time*?" Inés says. "What does that mean?"

They are walking up a cobblestone street and Miguel exaggerates the climb. Inés is behind him and he turns around. "It doesn't mean anything. We met her in the plaza, I think. Or maybe at Tabú? I can't even remember. She didn't matter."

Inés knows she's being irrational. She knows Miguel came here to have fun, and that's exactly what he's been doing. But it's that moment that she realizes she's falling in love with him. She knows because she has never before had this intense desire to erase a man's past.

"Calm down," Miguel says, laughing a little.

Inés balks. "Why don't you call me when you grow up?" she says. She turns around and walks toward the metro.

"Inés," Miguel calls. "Wait." But he doesn't follow her.

* * *

Miguel walks around for a bit, thinking Inés will come back or call him. But after an hour, she hasn't, and so he goes to a Turkish carryout and gets a kebab. He eats it and then orders one for Lautaro to go. Then he walks home.

Once at Lautaro's, he drops his keys on the table. "Miguel," Lautaro commands from the couch. "You have a visitor."

He looks up and sees an old woman. On the tall side, with chestnut curls and a slight frame.

She is well-dressed and unmistakably Argentine, and for a second Miguel worries that their father has had a heart attack and she is some distant relative or friend sent here to break the news.

He doesn't recognize that her mouth is nearly identical to his because she hasn't smiled yet. He hasn't noticed that her upper lip rises and reveals the same amount of gum that his does when he smiles.

She doesn't look up. She seems timid. Who is this old bat?

Miguel looks at Lautaro, who has stood up. Lautaro looks spooked.

"I brought you some food," he says, gesturing to the bag on the table. Lautaro won't meet Miguel's eyes and he doesn't look at the food. He stares in the woman's direction.

When he remembers it years later, he'll remember things that never happened. Like Lautaro meeting him at the door, squeezing his beefy frame through the slim opening and saying, *Vos preparate.* Get ready. He'll remember Inés calling him to make up from the fight and ignoring the call. He'll remember picturing his parents, his mother's blond hair and his father's white hair, looking so healthy and safe in their khaki pants and windbreakers. They're so reasonable! They've never made a sudden move in his life! A semi-translucent image of them pulsing in his head like a hologram, making it hard to see the old woman. They don't look upset or even resigned. They're just there. As they always have been. *Miguel,* they take turns saying. *Hijo. Los chicos.* The words will break apart in his head like pieces of stale bread.

But in the real life version, Lautaro's just standing there, looking stunned, staring at the old woman. And she, for her part, sits there staring at Miguel.

"*Buenas…?*" Miguel says uncertainly.

Lautaro takes an awkward step forward and gestures toward the woman. She stands up and comes closer. She has good posture.

"I'm your grandmother," she says. Her voice—steady, as though she were there in a professional capacity—makes her seem younger than she looks. "Your biological grandmother."

It hits him then that she is *his* biological grandmother, but not Lautaro's. He looks at Lautaro. It has clearly hit him too.

"You want me to leave?" Lautaro asks, the edge in his voice so subtle, it's almost indiscernible. Why is he angry? That the woman exists at all? This proof, finally here and materialized in ugly human form that they are not now, nor have they ever been, real brothers.

Or is it that someone has come to claim Miguel before Lautaro? Is he jealous? That can't be it—they've never been jealous.

"No," Miguel says. He wants him to stay. He wants Lautaro to stand next to him until this woman goes back to wherever she came from.

"What are you doing here?" He knows it's a rude question, but it just comes out.

The old woman steps closer to him, and Miguel steps behind the table with Lautaro. Laucha's bulk is doing no good. He might as well be a cornered animal, so uncomfortable does he look.

"My name is Beatriz Ferrero. I came here to meet you," she says. "And to tell you about your parents," she says. "My son Alejandro and daughter-in-law Sabina. Those are your parents' names."

Miguel laughs and it sounds mean. It feels mean. He looks next to him and Lautaro has gone.

"Laucha," he calls. It sounds weak.

His brother comes out from his bedroom wearing a coat. "I'm going to go," he says. His voice cracks. "I've got my phone."

And then he's gone.

And Miguel is alone with this woman. He doesn't know what to do.

"I know this is a surprise," Beatriz says.

Miguel gestures for her to sit back down. His body moving through the manners without consulting his brain. He sits across from her in the chair. "That's okay," he says. "I know I'm adopted."

"I'll be here for a few weeks," she says. "I know you'll need to get used to the idea of me." Her words are taken right from the script Mariela suggested. Beatriz had also been told to buy an open-ended ticket, because it could take the kid weeks.

Miguel nods. "Are you here alone?"

"I am," Beatriz says. "My husband—your grandfather—may come from Italy." She looks at her hands.

"He doesn't know I'm here yet."

Miguel feels an awful ache inside him. He realizes that he hates this apartment without Lautaro in it. Outside, the streets are noisy with people stopping for drinks on their way home from work. He hates Madrid, too, without Lautaro by his side to make fun of it. But wasn't that the problem with Buenos Aires as well? That Laucha was back in Patagonia finishing high school and dead set on going to Europe for university?

This woman is staring at him. "Can we meet for lunch tomorrow? Once you've had some time to rest? My treat." Beatriz has assumed that the boy is rich, given the apartment and the profile Mariela provided. But she doesn't want to leave room for any excuses.

Miguel agrees to lunch at the Italian-Argentinean restaurant down the street and reluctantly gives her his cell phone number. He accepts an awkward hug that lasts too long and a series of kisses like staccato notes on his cheek. When he pulls himself from her hug he sees that her cheeks are wet with tears. He asks her, hesitatingly, if she has a place to stay while in Madrid, and she assures him she does.

5

Beatriz arrives at the restaurant early. Miguel is twenty minutes late and he knows he looks like shit. He stayed up almost all night drinking alone. Lautaro hasn't come back to the apartment, and though he began dialing both Inés and his parents' numbers a handful of times, he never finished. What would he have said? He is angry at Laucha for not coming home, but if he had, what would they have said?

Beatriz stands up when he arrives and hugs him. He acquiesces, pats her back weakly.

"You look like your father," Beatriz begins as soon as they sit down. "Would you like to see some pictures of him?"

Miguel stares at her across the table.

He seems angry. Beatriz pulls a photo album from her bag and puts it on the table. "He was so excited about you," she says. She hears the words come out of her mouth and wishes her voice wavered. She wishes she had the ability to *sound* as emotional as she feels.

Miguel opens the menu, dismissing her. "Maybe later."

Beatriz nods. Mariela told her to be prepared to be rejected.

"Can you tell me a little bit about yourself?" She counts to five inside her head before continuing. "It means so much for me..." *Slow down*, she tells herself. *You'll overwhelm him*. "...to finally meet you. You remind me so much of my...son." She can't stop herself from saying it, even though Mariela had told her not to talk about Alejandro too much. He may not want to hear it.

"His name was Alejandro," Beatriz says. She is hoping to trigger Miguel's curiosity, but he only nods and studies the menu.

This name, this man who must look like him and in fact created him, but is now clearly gone, suppresses Miguel's appetite. Why did he agree to lunch with this woman? Why didn't he give her a fake number, go stay at a hotel, tell Lautaro she's a crazy? Be done with it?

"Why do you boys live here?" Beatriz asks.

The sound of her voice intensifies his hangover.

Miguel doesn't look up from the menu. "I'm on a year off. My brother's studying international business. We have a lot of family friends here." He runs his finger along the side of the menu, looks up at her impatiently.

"And Victor and Linda come and visit?" Beatriz was given the first names—first names only—of Miguel's adoptive parents. She knows she is far off the script. *Don't bring up his adoptive parents. Don't let on that you know who they are. It's a miracle those kids don't have bodyguards, given how loaded their father is.*

Miguel winces. He does not like the sound of his parents' names on this woman's lips. Does she know them? Does she know who his father is? Is she going to contact them? He cannot for the life of him imagine how his father would react.

Miguel looks up from the menu and shakes his head slowly, as though she were dull.

"And the holidays?" Beatriz presses. "Are you going back to Argentina or are they coming here?" The words come out of her mouth quickly. She wants to slow down, but she can't.

"Neither," Miguel says. "Lautaro and I may stay here, or we may go some place."

"They won't see you on Christmas?" She curses

herself. Her voice, she knows, is full of judgment.

Miguel smirks. "My father is older. He doesn't trav—"

"Stop," Beatriz interrupts.

Miguel stops talking. He raises an eyebrow.

She has never in her seventy-two years felt so out of control. Her life has been full of losses, some mundane, some extraordinary. One recalibrates to losses. But here is what she wants, right in front of her face. She wants to reach out and bring him to her, hug him until he sees what she sees, knows what she knows.

But her brain is running the show and it just keeps going.

"Your father. I know that you have a father and I'm sure he's wonderful."

Miguel purses his lips.

"But—your biological father, my son, he's—they're dead. Your biological mother, too."

Miguel's face clouds. He looks like he's in pain. But she can't stop herself.

"They were kidnapped by the government. Tortured and murdered." She can hear her voice rising. She takes a deep breath, slows down. "The way they killed them, there was no dignity. We were never given their bodies to bury."

"How do you know they were tortured?"

She doesn't answer. Whatever she was going to lose with this boy is already set in motion. She goes on.

"They kept your mother alive longer so you could be born. So you could be given to some government puppet as a bribe, a kickback—" Beatriz stops when she feels a hand on her shoulder. The waiter is behind her.

"Is everything okay, *señora*?"

Beatriz looks across the table at Miguel: his eyebrow is still raised; he's looking at her as if she were a child he was indulging. She excuses herself and goes to the bathroom. Mariela had tried to prepare her for this—that the child would use the word *parent* and it would infuriate her. She is standing in front of the mirror trying to regain her composure when it occurs to her that Miguel might leave. She rushes back to the table, where Miguel sits staring straight ahead.

She lowers herself into her seat. The waiter has filled their water glasses.

"I ordered you a maté," Miguel says. He seems pleased with his generosity.

Just get through this, man, he tells himself. Order quickly and get out. It occurs to him that while he has been treating Beatriz as just another elderly friend of his parents he has to be nice to, in reality his parents could not have a clearer enemy.

It occurs to Beatriz as well. "I'm sorry," she says. She forces herself to steer the conversation away from Victor and Linda. "It was very difficult for me to lose my son and daughter-in-law—"

"They were married?" Miguel asks.

He sounds surprised, interested. "Of course," Beatriz says. "They got married on a rainy day. It was pouring."

She doesn't tell him that she didn't actually go to the wedding; that Sabina was pregnant and Alejandro married her out of obligation. He said he loved her, that he wanted to marry her anyway. Beatriz told him he didn't have to. She'd taken the downpour on their wedding day as a bad omen. She offered him money for an abortion, because she secretly thought that the baby might not be his. Of course as soon as they were gone she abandoned that idea, but it had been in the back of her mind the whole time. Those subversive groups were known for sharing everything, and Sabina had been beautiful. Alejandro was too skinny, lacking Giancarlo's charm and gravitas, always trying too hard to make up for it with his arrogant nerdiness.

A small, suppressed grin begins to form on

Miguel's face and Beatriz realizes that he feels sorry for her. It settles on her like fog that he's a posh, futuristic version of Alejandro. For a second, Beatriz is proud that Alejandro had this arrogance, too. She hopes he gave the government hell every step of the way. She hopes he laughed in their faces, corrected their pronunciation, ridiculed their logical fallacies.

But there's something about Miguel that's better. It's undeniable. He's got better posture, better teeth. He's skinny like Alejandro was, but his shoulders are broader. His bones must be stronger. He's more relaxed, even while meeting her, than Alejandro was throughout his early manhood.

Damn the script. Damn Mariela. "What have your parents told you about my son and his wife?" It comes out as a challenge, but she doesn't care.

Miguel takes her measure, accepts her challenge with a flicker of his eyes. "Nothing," he says simply.

Nothing. The word clangs in Beatriz's head. Her grandson and his adoptive parents have discarded his parents as easily as the government did.

"They weren't nothing," Beatriz says. She tries not to sound too desperate. "Your father was intelligent, like you. He asked a lot of questions and he thought the world should be a fair place. The country was in tumult. Thousands of people had disappeared already. He met your mother at a meeting of young intellectuals. They were some of the people actually *doing* something about it—" she stops when she notices he's dipping bread in oil using his left hand.

"Are you left-handed?" she asks. Alejandro wasn't, but Giancarlo is and Beatriz's mother was.

Miguel's hand freezes near the plate. He doesn't want to give her any more ammunition.

"No," he says. He shakes his head and puts the bread down. "I'm sorry," he says, though he doesn't sound it. "I'm sorry I called your son nothing." He's got the manners of rich kids. The manners she had when *she* was a rich kid. Polite, but with a mechanical sincerity. Does he use this shit on other people? Does he think he's a European? Does it work? It must.

"They weren't criminals," Beatriz says. The waiter appears with the maté and a beer for Miguel. "I want you to know that."

"They talked too much," Miguel says. He offers it like a settlement. This kid is so spoiled he thinks there was a *right* way to overthrow a corrupt government. It angers Beatriz more than the *nothing* comment.

"I grew up in a time when having something to say was a good thing," she says. "Even so, I talked too much. At the dinner table, my father used to say, 'Do they not let you talk in school?'"

Miguel is giving her a vacant smirk across the table. She wants to say that, one day, if he is like her, words he didn't even know he knew would come out of his mouth and string themselves together in ways that feel totally out of his control. They'll hang in the air forever and make him detest himself, the way they have made her detest herself. They'll turn him into a hateful person, a wildly fresh and new person that even she—with all her overactive imagination that she'd been chastised for since she was little—could not have invented.

A person like her, who said things to Alejandro like *You can't trust her, a woman that beautiful. She'll betray you, sooner or later.* Things that drove Alejandro out of the house and further into the folds of the group.

And *Take this money. See what Sabina says when you offer it.* Alejandro took it and said, *I'll consider this your wedding gift. It's the least you could do, considering you couldn't be bothered to show up.*

And *Ciao, suerte.*

Which is what she said to Alejandro, without so much as a kiss on the cheek, on the last day she saw him.

* * *

Miguel lets Beatriz pay. He lets her kiss him on the cheek when they say goodbye. He takes down her address in Madrid and her address in Rosario. He takes down her phone number in Argentina. He doesn't offer anything of his own, any way for her to trace him once they're back in Argentina. He hails a taxi for Beatriz and tells the driver the name of her hotel. After he shuts the door Beatriz turns around, but Miguel has already begun to walk in the opposite direction.

6

Breakfast is served in the dining room, but Eduardo is never hungry until lunchtime. He turns on the television. A curly-haired blonde is reciting the news. She reminds him of someone. One of the detainees. He had preferred the females, gotten to know some of them. Nice girls who just got caught up with the wrong men. A shame. The newscaster nods her head and he realizes who she reminds him of. The one who'd given birth to the boy he'd given to Victor Alcorta Jones in Patagonia. The millionaire Eduardo had just about broken his back trying to get to donate to the effort in the Malvinas.

The girl's name was Sabrina. Or maybe Sabine? No, Sabrina. She had a head full of curly blond hair just like this newscaster and she was so weak by the time she went into labor that she wouldn't push. He had stood outside the infirmary, peeking in. He'd been telling the director of the center they needed a doctor round the clock, especially for moments like this, but he wouldn't listen.

Eduardo remembers Alcorta Jones' file well. A big target. And his, Eduardo's, responsibility to convince him. The guy was one of the wealthiest men on the continent. Had grown up privileged and studied in England, where he'd put together some dream team of Asian geniuses and African princes or something, and the group of them had gotten started in scrap metal and tongue depressors. He was involved in real estate development—the guy owned half of Patagonia—and he had a foundation for drinkable water in Africa. Another one to protect the Amazon. And a scholarship fund to send one deserving Argentine student to the London School of Economics every year. Jesus, Eduardo thought. This man. His official occupation as listed in the file was Venture Capitalist. Alcorta Jones had finally settled back in Patagonia, with all his money. Who better than a filthy rich Patagonian to set the example for funding the Malvinas cause?

The big question, especially with a surname like Jones, was: Did he love England? Did he support their absurd imperialistic claim to the Malvinas? It was unclear from the file how much time Victor had actually spent there. He'd grown up in Patagonia and had been investing in it from abroad for decades. Those were good signs. Fluent in English and Italian, proficient in French and Japanese. Newlywed. Really? At his age? The wife was an engineering professor at the new university in San Juan. A native Patagonian herself. And only a decade younger than him.

Eduardo contacted Victor and his people nearly every day for the first half of April, but Victor was elusive, evasive, and vague about his hope for the reclamation of the islands.

Eduardo couldn't seem to get anywhere. It was during this time that he began forgetting things again. He mixed up the names of his own daughters, who were living with his wife and her parents now while he slept in the barracks as though he were in basic training. He tried all the keys on his ring before finding the right one to open the barracks door. He would sit in front of his dinner and it wouldn't even look like food to him.

Eduardo called Victor the third week of April. The Royal Navy has so many allies, he said, and we have none. Don't you want your country to have what is rightfully hers? Don't you want Argentina to heal?

Eduardo was desperate to convince Victor. Victor was dismissive. He had just gotten married, he told

Eduardo. He and Linda would be going on a long honeymoon starting next week. He'd be out of the country. Helping this government is not exactly his first priority, he said. This government that taxed him so exorbitantly.

Another month would pass before Eduardo was finally able to unlock Alcorta Jones. At the Archdiocese in Buenos Aires, it was Sister Angela that alerted him to the fact that Alcorta Jones and his wife had been very generous with the church—so generous, in fact, that they were now near the top of the adoption waiting lists. He sat at his desk after that phone call, stunned by this new information, and felt the miracle form around him. It was the only word he could think of to describe the coincidence: miracle.

Victor, Eduardo thought to himself, and the hope he felt made his head clear. This was something bigger than the Malvinas, more permanent even than the land he lived to defend. *Victor, I may be able to help you.*

The next day he went to the detention center and saw Sabrina, a fierce blonde in what had to be the last trimester of pregnancy. He tried to befriend her, brought her hot tea one night before bed. She thanked him silently with her eyes and took it through the bars of her cell only to throw it right back at him, splashing the scalding water onto his uniform and burning his wrist and forearm. He didn't give up, though. The next day he left a little crate of cherries outside her cell and the following week he cornered her as she was coming out of the questioning room and handed her a still-warm empanada he'd wrapped in a napkin from his own lunch. She tried not to accept it, but he told her there was meat in it, and she kept it. Eduardo wasn't exactly Catholic and he wasn't exactly an atheist, but he liked to think he lived his life by a sort of universal golden rule, and there was a small part of him that felt responsible for the well-being of this unborn child, and even for this feral, lost woman. By then the paperwork was all arranged—Sabrina's child would be given to the Game Changer (as they'd begun calling him around the office) and his wife in Patagonia, and then she would be transferred.

When her time came it was as though she knew all about the plans to separate her from her child and wouldn't push him out. She *couldn't* push, though. Eduardo remembers that now in a moment of lucidity. The blonde on the news is joking with the other newscaster and smiling a big, generous smile and he remembers how one day he asked Sabrina to smile, told her he bet she had a beautiful smile, and would she smile for him just once? And she spat at him. The guard had threatened to beat her, but Eduardo had stopped him. For some reason she'd gotten under his skin, and when she couldn't push her own child out he'd felt for her. She'd been wailing earlier that day in her cell about her man who wasn't there anymore, and he'd tried to calm her, but had been unsuccessful. It was sad, but you couldn't have these people raising children.

When she passed out during labor, he began to panic. He'd promised a healthy baby to Victor. He'd told him he had a good feeling about a boy coming along, and you could tell this Sabrina had been good-looking before she got to the detention center. Better still, she had the same coloring as Victor himself. Victor would be able to pass the kid off as his own. Eduardo wanted a bonus for this. He wanted, at the very least, for Victor to acknowledge that he'd done a good job, that he had paid attention to these details.

7

Miguel doesn't go back to Lautaro's. What would he say?

He walks around Malasaña and goes to the Parque del Oeste. The sun sinks behind the suburbs and the sight of it depresses him. Couples hold hands and make out. Children shout and run around and play catch and all of this pisses Miguel off. He calls Inés. She picks up on the first ring and immediately apologizes. "Now you know," she says softly. "I'm a jealous person."

"I don't care about that," he says. He tells her about Beatriz, about lunch. About his biological parents.

Inés is speechless.

"I had a chance to find out about them. She brought pictures and everything, and I wouldn't let her show me. I was rude."

"You were in shock," Inés coos. "You can get in

touch with her back in Argentina." This is it, Inés realizes. It's the big thing she's been wanting to happen between her and Miguel. The thing that will tie him to her irrevocably.

"Get in touch with her back in Argentina?" Miguel repeats. He knows he can't betray his parents that way, as clearly and as certainly as he knows he disgusted Beatriz. I'll never know, he thinks. Unless, maybe, Beatriz outlives his parents? Unlikely. She looks almost as old as his father, and though he's old, the idea of him dying is unthinkable.

He lies back on the grass and a shiver seizes his body. For a second, it doesn't feel like his. He feels completely and totally displaced. Sometimes as a kid he would wake up in a hotel room on vacation with his family and not know where they were. In Geneva, in Tokyo, in Lima—his father and mother in one bed, snoring lightly, and Lautaro beside him, sucking his thumb. Now he feels that way in his own body. Where is he?

"What were they like?" Miguel asks Inés. His voice is desperate, thin. "I don't know anything about them. I never will. I lost my chance."

"Your mother," Inés begins, "was beautiful. She was the most beautiful woman in all of Rosario. All of Argentina. She looked like a Botticelli Virgin." It doesn't occur to Inés how cheesy, how clichéd the comparison is. She's recently taken an art history class and the Botticelli paintings were the only ones that didn't bore her, the only ones she can remember.

"Rosario," Miguel says, as though it's swear word. "I'm not from Rosario. I've never even been there."

"Shh," Inés says. "Your mother was so excited when she got pregnant with you. She knew you'd become who you are. She knew how intelligent you'd be, how handsome." She wants to tell him that she loves him, but she knows it will only turn him off.

Miguel doesn't say anything, but Inés can hear him breathing heavily. She can hear the sounds of kids playing.

"I've been everywhere," Miguel says. "I've been to the Berlin Wall and to Hong Kong. With my dad once. He took me and Lautaro along for a business trip." He's crying now. "I've been to fucking Iceland. But I've never been to Rosario."

"You turned out to be exactly who they would've wanted you to be."

Miguel knows that he didn't. He knows that Inés knows this, too, and Beatriz. He tries to sit up on the grass, but falls backward.

"Miguel?" Inés asks. "Are you there?"

He could go. To Rosario. When he gets back. He could do it. He's got a credit card, his own bank account. It's only a few hours from Buenos Aires. They'd never have to know. He exhales.

"Yes," he says to Inés, though he didn't hear her question.

8

Giancarlo hears the phone ring from the kitchen, but he doesn't rush to pick it up before the answering machine gets it.

"Giancarlo." Beatriz's voice sounds different from the last time they spoke, but he can't place how. "I found him. It's a boy." A pause. "Alejandro's child. I met him."

Giancarlo startles, drops his cigarette onto the newspaper he'd been reading, curses himself as he stamps it out. He shuffles his feet. Grandson. He feels a wave at the base of his skull like the beginning of a migraine, because now he must invent a person and then rush him through childhood, puberty, into, what? How old is he? Sabina had disappeared before she'd started showing and they never got an official date of death for her.

"How old is he?" he blurts out loud to the answering machine like an idiot.

"I'm in Madrid," Beatriz continues. "He looks like Alejandro. A little bit like you." He can hear that she's smiling, and this eases something that's been clenched inside of him for a long, long time.

Giancarlo is frozen. *Pick up the phone*, he wills himself. *Pick up the phone, and find out where this boy is, and—*

"He's left-handed," Beatriz is saying.

She saw him. She touched him.

"But he wouldn't admit to it, and he tried to cut his meat with his right hand, and…" she laughs and it sounds like her old laugh, the one he hasn't heard in years.

He can't speak. His throat is thick and then closed with what feels like a disease. He wants to see her. He aches to speak Spanish with her, to be alone in a car with her, to feel young and strong and to have hope for something. He begins to cry.

"He was adopted by some millionaire in Patagonia. He's a spoiled rich kid. He didn't care about Alejandro or Sabina. He won't meet me again, I can tell. Maybe he would meet you?" She sighs. "I just wanted to tell you. Call me back, if you can." She doesn't hang up right away and he feels self-conscious, like she can see him sitting there, listening.

"*Ciao, suerte*," she says and hangs up.

* * *

Beatriz barely unpacked, so it doesn't take much to organize her things. What a spoiled brat the kid is. She sits on the bed. She doesn't quite know what to do. She's been to Madrid before. She's seen the Prado, the Palace, the Retiro. She doesn't feel the need to stay and sightsee. She won't see the boy again, at least not here. She looks around the room. Outside a gray curtain descends on this foreign city. She finally found him. He is unmistakably Alejandro's, and, by extension, hers and Giancarlo's. She lies on the bed and puts her hand on her belly, where Alejandro once lived in his smallest form, and part of Miguel somehow too, inside Alejandro.

Giancarlo, she thinks. Maybe he'll call her back. Maybe not. He is living with his cousin Valentina, she knows. Valentina used to bother Beatriz, but not anymore. He never calls, just sends postcards every few months reporting the weather and minor health problems. Good for him. He has found something better than her relentlessness and is rewarded with happiness every day.

9

The next day is sunny but cold and Inés balls her hands into fists inside her coat pockets as she hurries across the bridge to the metro at Canillejas. It's after ten, but there are still plenty of people on the bridge. Headed to the center of the city to do holiday shopping, maybe, to interview for a job, to visit a parent or a grandparent. What would it be like in Buenos Aires? Did they have a metro, a good bus system? She knows Miguel can drive and even has a car there. Would she learn to drive or would she be able to do all her coming and going with him? She feeds her metro pass into the machine and pushes the rung of the turnstile forward with her hipbone. The car has arrived and is switching tracks. She takes a seat at the far end of the car, facing the rest of it. A pair of nuns, one elderly with glasses, the other one young with a pale, pimpled face, sit close to Inés. A middle-aged man in a windbreaker stares at the nuns and Inés. At Ciudad Lineal, a half-dozen Central American women get on. They don't speak to one another, but are clearly together, and Inés wonders if they came to Spain as a group or if they met here. When she walks around Buenos Aires, will people be able to tell that she's a foreigner? Once she starts talking, for sure. But just from looking at her?

At Pueblo Nuevo the car fills to the point of crowding and Inés gives her seat to an old woman with a cane. At Ventas it thins out, but she stays standing. *Makeup sex*? she is thinking. *Come with me to Argentina sex*? *Of course, Miguel, I love you sex*? Too soon for that? Probably. Inés is leaning into a pole, biting her lip, pondering game plans, when she sees her aunt Maria Elena come onto the car at Diego de Leon. Of course. What was a day without running into one of them? Javi and Juan at school. Rocío and Vanessa in the neighborhood. Elisa at Pacha the night she met Miguel there. Uncle Diego at the Corte Inglés. And Grandpa at the kiosk on Serrano until he died. Maria Elena zooms toward her as if there were magnets inside their stomachs drawing them together without their consent.

"*Hola, tía*," Inés says, leaning in to be kissed.

Maria Elena wants to know where she's going.

"Alonso," Inés tells her.

"Your boyfriend?"

"Malasaña."

Maria Elena nods. "You're going to walk?"

"It's only a few blocks."

"It's cold out."

Inés nods and looks at a place on the wall of the metro car just beyond Maria Elena's perfectly coiffed hair.

"And his secret grandmother? From Argentina? Is she still here?"

Madre mía. How did she know? Had her mother called her in the middle of the night? Not unthinkable.

"Are you going to meet her?" Aunt Maria Elena wants to know. She is a rigid, formal woman with upright posture, and Inés stands up a little straighter without meaning to.

"I don't know," Inés says. "I mean, eventually, I'm sure."

Maria Elena raises her eyebrows. She is perpetually underwhelmed, unimpressed with Inés, which makes her Inés's least favorite aunt. Everyone else is always praising her for how pretty she is, how easygoing, how much fun she is to be around.

"*Bueno*," Inés says somewhat helplessly. She kisses her aunt as the car slows to a halt at Alonso Martinez and walks off before Maria Elena's countenance can get under her skin.

The day has warmed up in the half hour she's been underground, and she takes a deep breath as she walks up the steps to the street. She makes her way down Santa Barbara to San Mateo. She knows Malasaña—she's been partying in its streets since she was thirteen—but having grown up in Canillejas, this neighborhood still feels somewhat foreign to her.

She rings Lautaro's doorbell and Miguel buzzes her up. She expects him to be waiting for her in the doorway, but he's not. The door is unlocked.

"*Hola*?" she calls as she opens it slowly, tentatively.

He's home alone. He's sitting on the couch with his knees spread wide, staring at the television.

Inés sheds her bag and coat and joins him on the couch.

He looks at her like nothing has happened. "*Buenas*," he says.

She thinks they'll kiss, but they don't. Miguel lays his head back so he's facing somewhere between Inés and the television. He exhales loudly.

Inés brings her knees to her chest and arranges herself to face him. "Tell me everything." Her voice is practically a whisper.

"I told you everything yesterday," he says.

Her face must register displeasure, because he shifts to face her, puts his hand on her foot and says a little more kindly, "There's nothing new to tell."

"Is she still here?"

Miguel shrugs. "I think so."

"Are you going to call her?"

He nods. "When I go back, yeah."

Inés is silent. It would be weird for him to ask her about Buenos Aires now. It'll be months. Other things have to happen before then.

"And Laucha?" she asks.

He looks at her like *Laucha what*?

"Did he meet her? What does he think?"

Miguel nods and tells her that Lautaro met the woman briefly. He says Lautaro, not Laucha, and it feels pointed. Inés feels a flash of embarrassment at using his brother's nickname and almost automatically imagines what her nosy family would say about the situation she finds herself in:

Inés has never been in love before. Inés *has* been in love before, with Javi. Inés was not in love with Javi, *por favor*. She just lost her virginity to him, that's all. Inés is afraid. What's she going to do in Argentina? In the frozen tundra, no less? Without her mother, without Julia, who's been nipping at her heels her entire life?

Inés shivers. Running into her aunt Maria Elena messed her up, made her lose her confidence right at this important moment when she needs to be here with Miguel. She pushes her family's voices out of her head. Sits next to Miguel on the couch. Watches him pretend to watch television. Watches him check his phone. Checks her own phone.

"Your finance exam?" Miguel asks when the TV show cuts to a commercial break.

"It's tomorrow."

Miguel is silent for a moment. "You're prepared?"

Inés nods. He wants her to leave. Should she? Or should she stay and push?

She looks at him. "There's a study group meeting this afternoon. I could go. It wouldn't hurt."

Miguel nods approvingly.

They sit awkwardly and watch TV for another couple of minutes, and then Inés stands to go. She gathers her things and says, "*Bueno.*" The look on Miguel's face is one of extreme boredom masking extreme fear. Inés knows this look because she has seen it on herself for years. But the fear—the fear of nothing, the fear of falling and falling and never hitting the ground—lessened when she met Miguel, and she is deeply, viscerally offended that he doesn't feel it too.

He kisses her at the door and it feels dead.

She says, "You call me if you…if anything—"

Miguel nods and kisses her again and it feels a little less dead. They say goodbye and she heads back out into the street. There is no study group, and though her finance exam is in fact the next day, she has studied all she's going to and will probably fail it again. Who cares? She'll take it again next semester with a teacher who can actually teach. She makes her way back toward Alonso Martinez. Things die briefly and come back to life all the time, she tells herself. Wasn't her mother always telling her how many times she and her father broke up before they got serious?

When she arrives at the metro stop at Alonso Martinez, she realizes she doesn't want to go underground. Doesn't want to go home and explain to her mother, to Julia, the nothingness that just occurred.

She walks down Génova to the Plaza de Colón. She sits and watches the skateboarders. Her brother and his friends come here. It occurs to her that she's never actually seen Miguel move his body, for all the exotic sports he's told her he plays. Inés has never been skiing, let alone snowboarding. She's been on a horse just once, as a child, and the idea of hunting grosses her out.

She stands to go, thinking she'll head home. Julia's home studying, and Pablo will be home from school soon. Her mother will make a special lunch. She can tell her mother quickly to leave it alone, and then she won't have to talk about it or answer any stupid questions and she can tell her mother off for blabbing to Aunt Maria Elena, too. She could do all of this, and she would probably feel fortified enough to call or at least text Miguel later on, and things might have changed by then.

She walks in through the door of her house. Julia is at the dining room table studying. Pablo is not there. Her mother is clearing the table around Julia.

"*Hola*," they say.

"*Hola*," she says back. Inés can feel her mother's eyes on her as she hangs up her coat, drops her bag and walks toward the stairs.

"Are you hungry?" her mother asks.

"No," Inés says.

"Did you eat with Miguel?"

"Yes," Inés says, annoyed, and her mother says quietly, almost so she can't hear, "There's pasta Bolognese."

Inés turns around. It's her favorite. "Fine," she says.

Her mother brings the bowl of pasta out along with some salad and the remainder of the baguette they'd eaten earlier. She lights a cigarette. Julia, who usually makes a face and a big show of coughing, doesn't look up.

Inés's phone buzzes on the table. She grabs it. A text message from Miguel. She doesn't want to open it here, for fear she won't be able to hide her reaction to whatever he says, and this will be the perfect opening for her mother to lay siege.

"Are you going to get it?" Julia finally speaks.

"Later," Inés says. "When I'm done eating."

She finishes the pasta and the three of them sit in silence. She stands to take her plates to the kitchen, but her mother waves her hand. "Leave it," she says. "I'll take care of it."

Inés puts the plates down and picks up her phone. She'll take it to her room and read it there. Or maybe she'll go out again. Maybe Miguel wants to see her.

"Are you okay?" her mother asks. Inés looks down to see her hand holding the phone shaking lightly. Julia is looking at her too. For an instant Inés feels pity for Miguel, for surely there is no way he shares this kind of telepathy with his parents or even Lautaro. Then she scolds herself for pitying him.

"Inés," her mother is saying. Julia looks alarmed. Inés looks down. She's dropped the phone. Her mother bends to pick it up. Inés doesn't stop her. Her mother gently presses the key on the phone to read the text message. Inés doesn't stop her. It's probably nothing—an apology for being weird before, an invitation to come over after her exam tomorrow, maybe, a silly joke about something he's seen in the plaza. One of his light digs about Spaniards, intended to provoke her into a text conversation that'll go on until they go to sleep at night. But Inés can't move. Her mother reads the message. Her face remains calm, betrays nothing. Inés doesn't want to read it, to know if she's at the beginning or the end.

Acknowledgements

I would like to thank Deena Drewis, whose intelligence and talent made this book so much better, and whose editorial eye and generosity changed the way I see fiction. So many thanks to the best writing group in the world: Jenny Patton, Molly Patterson, Samara Rafert, MaryKatherine Ramsey, and especially Ali Salerno for reading the early drafts and being such a profound network of support. My deepest gratitude to Derek Palacio for believing in me and this project even when I didn't believe in it myself; to Edan Lepucki for your support; to Beth Breese for being there for me, over and over and over; to Claire Watkins for your awesome friendship; to Harvey Grossinger and Kermit Moyer for encouraging me in the beginning; to Erin McGraw, Lee Abbott, Lee Martin and especially Michelle Herman, for teaching me so much, and to Michelle for continuing to mentor me long after she had to; to Will Moreton for giving me a job and a good reason to stay in Madrid for so long; to Los Quijotes for providing me a real family while I was there, especially Jose Antonio, Kory, and Juan; to my parents, Katie & John, Matt & Jess, and all the McGreevy's for your love, support, and encouragement; and finally, most of all, to Cami Freeman, whose intelligence, patience, faith, and friendship I couldn't have dreamt up if I tried, and without whom this story surely wouldn't have seen the light of day.